If Only We Had a Helicopter

If Only We Had a Helicopter

Roger McGough

With illustrations by
Michael Broad

Barrington Stoke

First published in 2015 in Great Britain by
Barrington Stoke Ltd
18 Walker Street, Edinburgh, EH3 7LP

www.barringtonstoke.co.uk

This story was first published in a different form in
Stowaways (Viking Kestrel, 1986)

Text © 1986 Roger McGough
Illustrations © 2015 Michael Broad

The moral right of Roger McGough and Michael Broad to
be identified as the author and illustrator of this work has
been asserted in accordance with the Copyright, Designs and
Patents Act, 1988

A CIP catalogue record for this book is available
from the British Library upon request

ISBN: 978-1-78112-463-5

Printed in China by Leo

For you, the reader

CONTENTS

Chapter 1

Take Your Puppies Home

One day was just like any other day. And the next wasn't.

One day I got up, had my breakfast and went to school. I came home, had my tea, went out to play with my best mate Midge, came home and went to bed.

The next day was almost the same until I came home from school. There in the kitchen was a shivering lump of a little thing. A bundle of black and white hair with a stubby tail at one end and a shiny black nose at the other.

You've guessed.

It wasn't a hippo or an elephant. It wasn't a snake or a baby giraffe. It wasn't even a kitten.

It was a dog. Dog.

D-O-G spells what it was.

It was love at first sight. As soon as I walked into the kitchen, the D-O-G opened his eyes, waggled to his feet and trotted over to me. I was so surprised I just stood there with my mouth open. He looked up at me and wagged his tail. It was as if he had been waiting for me all his life. If I'd had a tail I would have wagged it as well.

Instead, I picked him up and hugged him. I ran with him into the living room where we rolled around on the carpet and chased each other and played puppy games until Dad made me sit down for tea.

It turned out that one of my dad's friends had a dog that had just had puppies. It wasn't Christmas, or within shouting distance of my birthday, but Dad had still chosen one of the litter as a present for me.

That's a silly word to describe new-born puppies, isn't it? 'Litter.' It makes them sound like rubbish. Imagine the adverts –

"Keep Britain Tidy – Take your puppies home with you."

"Penalty for dropping puppies – £25."

And so on.

Chapter 2

Give a Dog a Name

Dad had to shout to get me to the table, but in the end, I sat down and had my tea.

After tea I didn't go to see Midge. I spent the evening with my new 4-legged mate instead. We wrestled and chased and tug-of-warred.

That night I dreamed exciting doggy dreams starring "Me and My Dog".

In one dream, I was shipwrecked and My Dog saved me from drowning. He took me by the collar and swam to a desert island.

In another, My Dog jumped in the window of a burning house and dragged me to safety.

In another, Me and My Dog chased and nabbed a gang of bank robbers.

It was all very life-like and hard work. As you can imagine, when I got out of bed in the morning I was dog tired.

That's another funny saying, isn't it? Because all the dogs I know are very lively. They're never too tired to go for a run or chase cats. Even old dogs who should know better.

I told Midge all about My Dog in Art class. Mrs Fowler heard me and she made me stand up in front of the class and tell everybody.

I hate doing things like that most of the time, but for once I quite enjoyed myself. Everyone was interested, even Polly Gibbs. She thinks she's so clever, and she isn't. Well she is, but she's hopeless at football.

When I told them I hadn't given the dog a name yet, Mrs Fowler became quite excited. For the rest of the afternoon all the class had to draw My Dog and describe him in their own words. For homework we all had to think up a good name for him.

4 p.m. couldn't come fast enough. But at last it did, just like it always does, dragging its feet. Midge and I were eager for doggy larks and we raced home like the wind. In fact, we were so fast we left the wind standing at the school gates.

Chapter 3

Jam Butties

When Midge and I got to our house there was nobody in. I had my own key so I opened the front door. I was expecting My Dog to jump up at and bark at me. But no. There was no yelp of welcome. Nothing.

"Here, boy," I called. No reply. We went in. My Dog wasn't in the kitchen or the living room.

"I hope he hasn't sneaked upstairs into one of the bedrooms," I said. "Dad warned him about that."

"I expect that's where he is," Midge said. He didn't sound very confident.

My Dog wasn't there.

"Maybe your mum's taken him out for a walk," Midge said.

"She's at work this afternoon," I said. I tried to make my voice sound normal even though my stomach was reaching up and trying to grab it.

When we went back into the kitchen to search for clues, we saw that the window was open.

"That's funny," I said. "No one ever leaves the window open." A horrible thought put its hands around my throat. "A burglar must have broken in and stolen him," I gulped.

"Burglars don't steal dogs," Midge said.

"Dog burglars do," I said. "You've heard of cat burglars, so there must be dog burglars too."

"Let's take a look outside," Midge said. "In case he's climbed out and got lost."

We searched the yard and the garden. That didn't take long. Then we searched at the next-door neighbours. No luck. So we decided to widen our search. Just as we turned into Beach Road, we met three boys from our class.

One of them was Wayne, a boy who was as bossy as boots. He also watched too much American TV and wanted to be a sheriff when he grew up.

Wayne pushed his shades up off his eyes. "What we've got to do," he said, "is to form a posse. Round up as many kids as we can and scout around. Everyone split up and tell another kid, and they've got to tell somebody else, and so on. That way we can get all the kids in the area out on the streets searching."

Wayne turned to me, clapped his hand on my shoulder and looked me straight in the eye. I could almost hear theme music swelling in the background.

"Don't worry," Wayne said. "We'll get your dawg back for you, if it's the last thing we do." He then turned and galloped down Beach Road and into the sunset.

Now we had others to help search the streets, Midge and I went back to the house. We could start there and work outwards. Also, we needed glasses of milk and jam butties to build up our stamina.

Chapter 4

The Heart not the Ear

Midge and I were in the kitchen, munching our butties and slurping our milk, when we heard a strange noise. At first, I thought it was Midge's tummy, but it wasn't. It was like a whimper wrapped in tin foil.

A dog sound was what it was, and a dog in need of help. Before you could say "Up in a flash," Midge and I were up in a flash. We searched everywhere.

In the cupboards.

Under the oven.

In the oven.

Under the cupboards.

In the fridge.

Under the sink.

Nothing.

We stopped rushing around and listened. It came again. A faint, pathetic cry that you heard with your heart not your ear. There was no doubt about it – the noise was coming from outside.

Midge and I opened the back door and stepped out. This time we didn't rush about in a state of panic, we just stood still and listened for a few minutes. And what we heard was silence. Just the sound of our own breathing. And then it came again.

Midge and I looked at each other with wide eyes, and then at the old coal bunker under the kitchen window. This was a heavy wooden box, about the size of a small fridge and with a sloping lid. It hadn't been used since long before I was born. But I opened it, and there he was. He was black as the coal he lay on, sad and shivering. My Dog.

I lifted him out and hugged him and
hugged him. Then Midge hugged him and we
all hugged each other until we were all black
with coal dust from the bunker. That's when
Mum and Dad arrived home.

One hour and 24 gallons of hot water later, we all gathered in the living room to discuss the afternoon's adventure. It turned out that Mum was the culprit who had left the kitchen window open. Dad owned up that he had opened the lid of the old coal bunker the night before to stash some garden rubbish in it.

It seemed the puppy was keen to explore the outside world. At some point he had climbed first a chair ...

then onto the kitchen table ...

then onto the bread bin ...

then out the open window, and

then up into the old coal bunker which slammed shut.

It must have been a terrible couple of hours trapped in the dark. But My Dog

seemed none the worse for his bad day as he chased around the room after my dad's slipper.

Sometimes I think a dog's memory only stretches as far back as its last meal.

Chapter 5

Bunker

First thing next morning, Mrs Fowler got me out again in front of the class to tell the story. At the end of it everyone clapped and went "Ah". Even Polly Gibbs, who isn't bad at football really.

Then, one by one, they had to call out the name they had chosen for My Dog.

"Bonzo," Blake said.

"Scamp," Sasha said.

"Rover," Rory said.

"Mac," Mo said.

And so on, and so on.

When everybody had finished I told them that the little dog had already chosen its own name. And when I told them what it was, they all agreed that there could be no other.

Bunker.

I admit that it's not a very doggy name. But it fitted somehow. And it still does.

Though Bunker never went in that dark old coal bunker again.

Chapter 6

Real Viking Warriors

The next day was a Wednesday. And that morning, Vikings raided the school.

Fierce men with red beards appeared from the back of the hall. They waved heavy swords and axes, and they ran between the rows of children, yelling and clanking.

Of course they didn't fool me for a minute. I knew real Viking warriors wouldn't have false beards – or yellow and blue trainers. But they looked real enough to make most of the kids scream and get excited.

At last the Head Teacher calmed everybody down and explained. They were a theatre group. Two of them turned out to be girls, which just goes to show what a big helmet and a blood-stained axe can do for you.

They all said hello, and told us that they were touring schools with a play about life in Liverpool when the Vikings arrived, thousands of years ago. It was really interesting to learn about the Viking invaders, and the Anglo-Saxons who had lived in the area, and the Romans who came later and set up their garrisons. I looked with new eyes at the kids around me. I could imagine them as the children of Saxon farmers or Roman soldiers. That made them all seem a lot more interesting.

That Wednesday morning was one of the best times I ever had in school. It made normal lessons seem boring. Midge agreed, and he was all fired up by the thought of becoming an actor. What he wanted to do when he grew up was to be a member of a theatre group which visited schools and chased children with large swords. I had to agree it was a good idea. To be an adult and get paid for dressing up and playing soldiers seemed as good a job as there could be.

Chapter 7

Gangsters in the Sky

Half-term came at the end of that week. It was October, and that October was a bully. It wore a grey frown and kicked the leaves about. It shook the trees and it banged on the windows. But it was just bluster.

The real tough guys, January and February, could be really mean when they wanted to. No sooner is Christmas over than they're up there in the sky like gangsters, armed with snow bullets and winds tipped with ice.

October may be loud, but it's usually dry. So Midge and I were able to go out every day. We played footy in the park with other lads who lived near by, or we took Bunker for long runs along the canal bank.

The days sped by, but on Friday we felt like doing something different. Midge had the brilliant idea of getting the train out to Formby then walking back along the shore.

"What we need before we go back to school," he said, "is buckets full of sea air."

So, we set off at about 10 a.m., with our rucksacks packed with jam butties, dog biscuits and pop. An hour later we were heading into the hilly sand dunes along the north shore from Liverpool. When you cross the dunes you come to a flat beach that stretches out to the Irish Sea. Miles and miles of nothing but miles and miles.

We sat on the tough grass on the highest dune we could find and ate our sarnies and drank our pop. Bunker was too busy chasing seagulls, so we saved his lunch for later.

In summer, the place would have been chock-a-block with day-trippers and smooching couples. But that day, thanks to grumpy October, we had the dunes to ourselves.

At first, we were Viking raiders, making mincemeat out of the Anglo-Saxons. Then

we were commandos, sneaking up on enemy soldiers and throwing grenades into their dug-outs. At long last, we were worn out. We had wiped out the German Army, two Roman legions and countless invaders from outer space. And we three brave warriors – well, two and a half really – headed down onto the shore and in the direction of home.

Chapter 8

Black and White Wind

Far, far ahead, Midge and I could see the lights, giant cranes and tower blocks of Liverpool. A cloud of grey hovered in the sky above the city, like a bad mood. Across the river on the far side was Birkenhead. Behind that, like a faint pencil drawing, we could see the mountains of Wales.

But when we stopped to look out to where the River Mersey runs into the Irish Sea, no land could be seen. Only ships returning tired to port across the bottle-grey waters, or others setting out with their spirits high, to see the world.

"Why don't we run away to sea again, Midge?" I said.

Midge shook his head. "Nah. I'm going to be an actor. Then I can get a part as a sailor in a film. That way I won't get seasick either."

"Being an actor's not the same as being a real sailor," I argued.

But Midge wouldn't have it.

"Anyway, you can't run away to sea now," he said, as he stooped to pick up a small piece of wood.

"Why not?" I asked.

Midge didn't say anything. Instead, he threw the stick out into the waves that rolled noisily onto the sand.

The answer to my question bounded in to fetch it. Of course, Bunker. I couldn't leave him! Mum and Dad would understand that I needed to go off in search of adventure – well, at least I hope they would – but not Bunker. There are some things you just can't explain to dogs.

We walked off faster then, because we were tired and hungry, and home seemed a long way off.

Only Bunker was still full of beans. He streaked across the sand this way and that, flapping like a piece of black and white wind.

And of course it was Bunker who found the buried treasure.

Chapter 9

X Marks the Spot

Bunker was sniffing around something that looked like a small, black pyramid in the sand. His barks were so loud that Midge and I broke into a run. As we got closer, we could see that the black shape was a box, half buried in the sand. The waves had dumped it there, and now they were bored. They were pulling away to go home to bed.

All thoughts we'd had of home were now forgotten. We scooped out the wet sand and dug and tugged with the superhuman force we saved for special occasions. Soon we

were able to pull the box free and look at our prize. It was made of black, rusted metal, and it was about the size of the chest that Long John Silver and the pirates fight over in 'Treasure Island'.

Our heads were still full of the Viking play from the week before, and of course we were sure the box contained Viking treasure. Perhaps one of their ships had gone down in a storm after a raid on Liverpool. Now, hundreds of years later, the sea was giving away one of its dark secrets.

Midge and I dragged the box up the beach and away from the sea's clutches. We couldn't wait to open it.

We would run our fingers through the heavy gold coins ...

We'd try on the golden crowns ...

We'd fling sapphires and rubies into the air ...

We'd find diamonds that would out-twinkle the stars that were taking root in the sky ...

The trouble was, we couldn't get the box open. There was no lock, but the lid was sealed shut. No matter how hard we tried – and we tried for ages – we couldn't prise it open. Of course, we didn't have the proper tools. What we had were bits of bricks and metal and wood that were lying around.

"A hammer and chisel, that's what we need," I said.

Midge nodded. "Either that or a few sticks of dynamite."

Bunker wagged his tail in agreement. I suppose he thought the box would be full of Dog Treasure like juicy bones, crunchy biscuits and huge hunks of meat. As if.

"Well, we can't drag this all the way home," Midge said. "And we won't be able to come back tonight with a hammer and chisel. So what do we do?"

"What we do," I said, "is bury the box for now and then come back tomorrow with the proper tools."

Midge agreed. "But let's be careful where we bury it, so that we can find it again," he said.

We decided it would be safer to bury our box of treasure in the sand dunes and away from the beach. No one would notice us digging there.

The box was as heavy and hard to move as a dead camel. The handles were stuck fast, and so we had to push, shove and drag it up and down the hills of shifting sand. At last we found the perfect hiding place. It was a deep hollow, so secret and safe that no one would stumble across it in a million years. Except us of course. And to make sure that we could, Midge and I stood with our backs to the sea and took our bearings.

It was almost dark now, but we could still make out a clump of pine trees to the left and a long low building ahead. To the right, there was a line of yellow lamps that twinkled above a road like an unfastened necklace.

We dug a hole about a metre deep, heaved in the box and covered it with sand. To mark the spot, we made the letter X with sticks, bricks and leftover summer litter.

"X marks the spot," Midge said when at last we had finished. "Goodnight, sweet treasure. See you in the morning."

Then off we set for home. It was cold now, and dark as a shadow's shadow. But we didn't care. We were rich, we were famous. No more jobs for Mum or Dad. No more bus passes for Midge's gran. For Bunker, a fairy-tale kennel, with a lamp-post in every room and a bone-shaped swimming pool in the garden. We would buy ships to stow away in, schools to skip off from.

In next to no time – which is no time at all – we were home.

Chapter 10

Bold as Brass

Saturday did not turn out as planned.

Midge and I both got home so late the night before that the grown-ups were up the wall. I could always tell when my dad was only pretending to be angry. He would put on his shouty voice and I would pretend to be sorry. But this time he was upset, and so was Mum. And his shouty voice was real because it came from deep inside him.

Midge and I couldn't tell them the real reason we were so late, because the treasure

47

was going to be a big surprise. I made up a fib about getting lost. Then I said I was sorry I had upset them – which I was – and then I went off to bed.

Next day, I wasn't allowed out at all.

Midge called at around 12, but I told him to keep away and lie low until Sunday. I hoped Mum and Dad would have forgotten about it all by then, even if they hadn't forgiven me. And they did. Even the sun came out to celebrate, bright and bold as brass. I've noticed that the sun often does that, the day before you go back to school.

Chapter 11

The Old Sneak Thief

On Sunday night Midge had had one of his brilliant ideas.

The brilliant idea was for us to ride out to Formby on our bikes, open the box with a hammer and chisel, and either

(a) bring back the booty in our bike bags

or

(b) rest the box – if we failed to open it – across both bikes and wheel it home.

Brilliant.

As Bunker didn't have a bike to ride, he had to stay behind while Midge and I pedalled off on our great adventure. We rode along the coast road to Southport, with a fresh wind behind us, to push us along. It was quite an impatient wind, in fact.

In no time at all – which is next to no time – we turned left off the main road, into Formby village, past the railway station and onto the track that leads down into the sandy hills. The only way we could go on here was to pick up our bikes and stagger up and down the dunes until we reached the firmer sand near the sea. There we got back on the bikes and cycled along in search of the spot where Bunker had discovered the box.

We half hoped that the footprints we had left would still be waiting for us, eager to show us the way. But no such luck. The sea, the old sneak thief, had nipped in overnight and taken them. I wondered what the sea did with all those footprints it stole from the shore. Are they all neatly piled up on the ocean floor somewhere, waiting for their owners to come and collect them?

We stopped when we thought we recognised part of the beach where the box had been washed up, and we turned left into the sand dunes. We followed what we hoped was the path we had taken. We humped the bikes onto our backs again and staggered up and down in search of the spot marked X.

It was still half-term, and sunny into the bargain, and so there were quite a few people about – joggers, dog walkers, kids playing football. They must have thought we were very odd.

After ten minutes of slithering and sliding, we collapsed into two tangled heaps.

"Whose brilliant idea was it to bring the bikes?" I said.

Midge looked glum.

"They're slowing us down too much," I said, "and we can't leave them anywhere in case they get pinched."

Midge shook some sand out of his ear and said nothing. Then his face lit up.

"I've got a brilliant idea," he said. "Why don't we bury the bikes here, mark the spot with an X, and then when we've found the box, come back and dig them up. Brilliant."

I looked at him to see if he was being serious. "Are you being serious?" I asked.

Midge's face broke into a grin. I jumped on him and tried to push his face into the sand, but I was laughing too much.

We rolled around then, fighting and giggling until at last we lay on our backs dizzy and panting. The sky above spun slowly round and round.

"If only we had a helicopter," I said, "we'd find the treasure in a couple of minutes."

"But we haven't," Midge said. "So it's no use thinking about it."

It was my turn for a brilliant idea. "Let's start again," I said. "But this time we'll take it in turns. One looks after the bikes while the other searches."

Chapter 12

Heavy Hearts and Heavy Shoes

And that's just what we did. We searched. For hours.

One sat on the beach and minded the bikes, while the other went inland and did the search. But not only were we unable to find the X, we couldn't even recognise the landmarks that we had chosen to give us our bearings. There were clumps of pine trees everywhere and lots of low buildings in the distance, with roads running every which way.

Everything looked so different in the light. And, of course, we couldn't wait until it got dark. Not with all the trouble we had caused the last time. So, we biked home with heavy hearts and heavy shoes – which were full of sand. The shoes, that is, not the hearts.

The ride back was murder. We were now fighting against a wind that seemed determined not to let us past. Most of the journey was spent in silence. Our heads were down, our legs were pumping away.

But as we neared home, the wind stood back and let us past. At last, we were able to sit up in our saddles and get our breath back. I said to Midge that we should tell the grown-ups about the treasure. We were back at school the next day, so it was important that they were let into the secret. My dad could organise a proper search party, with his friends from work. He might even be able to fly a helicopter. Midge agreed that made good sense. And so, as soon as we got back to mine, we told Mum and Dad the whole story.

When we had finished telling them, we thought that Dad would smile a proud smile and shake our hands. Mum would hug and kiss us, and tears of joy would stream down her cheeks.

"What clever boys!" they would say.

"That Viking treasure will make us richer than our wildest dreams," they would cry. "What clever, clever boys!"

But it wasn't like that. Not like that at all. Mum went pale and Dad began shouting. It wasn't the sort of shouting that came from deep inside. It was the sort that he did when he wanted you to listen. The shouting didn't last long, but the lecture that followed it did.

The lecture was all about poisons and bombs and other nasty things left over from

old wars. And about how when Dad was a
boy one of his friends had his hand blown off
when he opened a box on the beach. "There
are horrible accidents, even worse than that,
every year," he said. "Even now those old
World War Two bombs turn up all the time."

When he had finished, Midge and I were paler than Mum. Then Midge had another of his "brilliant" ideas. "Maybe if we told the police, we might get a reward," he said. "Or even get on the front page of the paper."

For the first time that night, Dad smiled.

"I don't know about the paper, but there wouldn't be any reward," he said. "Sorry, Midge. You could report it to the police, but the problem would be finding it. You see, those sand dunes may look like mini mountains but they're not. They're made out of sand and they shift and move whenever the wind blows. The X that you made will have vanished for ever. And the box? Well, it may turn up again one day. And if it does, let's hope that the next person to find it has got more sense than you two. Viking treasure indeed!"

The next day was school again as usual, and Midge and I heard no more about the box after that. There was nothing on TV about bomb blasts on Formby beach. No reports in the paper of Viking treasure.

It must be buried still beneath the sand. That box of dark secrets, waiting to be opened.

Our books are tested
for children and young people by
children and young people.

Thanks to everyone who consulted on
a manuscript for their time and effort in
helping us to make our books better
for our readers.

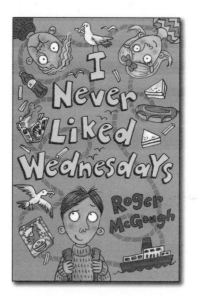

It was a Wednesday if I remember rightly.
I never liked Wednesdays for some reason.
I could never spell 'Wednesday' for a
start. And it always seemed to rain on
Wednesdays. And there were two days to
go to the weekend.

ISBN: 978-1-78112-462-8